CHRONICLES
FROM A
MYTH-STICAL
WORLD

CHRONICLES FROM A MYTH-STICAL WORLD

JEFFREY R. ROMANYSHYN

iUniverse, Inc.
Bloomington

CHRONICLES FROM A MYTH-STICAL WORLD

iUniverse books may be ordered through booksellers or by contacting:

iUniverse
1663 Liberty Drive
Bloomington, IN 47403
www.iuniverse.com
1-800-Authors (1-800-288-4677)

ISBN: 978-1-4620-4760-4 (sc)
ISBN: 978-1-4620-4761-1 (ebk)

Printed in the United States of America

iUniverse rev. date: 09/27/2011

CONTENTS

ASTRONOMER CARL

COACHMAN/SHERIFF

NARRATOR

OLD COUNTRY GRAY

Astronomer Carl/Coachman-Sheriff/Narrator/Old Country Gray

**Old Irish Grand Muse/Strong Hands/Tiny Dignity/
Twin Boy**

TWIN GIRL

VILLAGE IDIOT

WIFE OF THE
NARRATOR

Twin Girl/Village Idiot/Wife of Narrator

Cathedral Caretakers

Evil Wizard

Gatekeeper

Man Applying for Teaching Position

Money Bags

Preacher

Strong Hands Wife

Village Healer

VILLAGE MIDWIFE

WIFE ALLEGED PLAGIARIZER

Village Midwife/Wife of Alleged Plagiarizer

Woman Applying for Teaching Position

Foreword to *Chronicles From a Myth-stical World*
by Jeffrey Romanyshyn.

Foreword

A simple and pervasive warmth attends this poem of just under one hundred pages. For its length, the Table of Contents is quite complex, with many small bits coalescing into an organic whole to give the reader the arc of a sustained and coherent story, even though it is wrapped in a dreamy atmosphere within a place of the imagination made local and full of color.

I found that the quatrains consisting of two rhyming couplets, as in one of its opening units of rhyme offers a unique perspective:

So upon a window I limp to lean,
And cast my gaze upward: what do I gleam?
For a moment by two panes I'm confused,
Then first fact gained as I clear glass look through. (1)

The reader notices as well the split line demarcation that throws off the lines just enough to pull the eye along the left ragged margin. One notices as well how, in the spirit of Emily Dickinson, there is a reversal of word order as well as words left out in a poetic shorthand, requiring the reader to relinquish one's normal mode of organizing words into thoughts, as in "first fact gained as I clear glass look through." After a time, one adjusts to this off-center form of expression that actually matches the imaginal world created through the narrative. Poetically, the displaced words capture the dreamscape that the poem moves through, containing its own logic but with a twisted and torqued reality mirrored in the lines. As such, the lines beg to be read aloud, to hear the torque, to feel it in the eyes, mouth and ears.

At its heart, *Chronicles* accomplishes just that: it tells the story of the narrator, now an old man, who has gifted the editor with this manuscript with the caveat that it be read aloud, performed, made into a dramatic happening rather than a remembered story. We unwrap the manuscript with the recipient and read along, preferably aloud, as instructed. We learn that this is a hero's journey into the terrain of the imagination; where else might we find a tavern called "The Poetic Inn"? It is the voice of the narrative poet recounting his transformation, with the help of a bevy of characters, into a teacher at a university, a more formidable versifier, as well as a married man with children, one a foundling who seems to be from another galaxy, with powers and precociousness to match his strange birth.

The conflict arises with the mention of evil wizards (14) who must be conquered. The weapons of choice become those of music and song, a poetics of persuasion. And, like the inversion or reversal of words in the quatrain, the village the narrator enters will one day be ruled by the village idiot, who possesses more wisdom than the hordes combined.

How fortunate is this poet as well, for he meets and marries a beautiful young woman who supports him in his calling as poet. Some of the best lines occur to describe simple acts, as this:

The next morning early I do arise,
Softly from our bed, blankets barely sigh.
My wife's body shifts a slight position.
On with my robe I enter the kitchen.

Other delights include the name of the school he teaches at: Muse University (Muse You?) and the name of the foundling, Tiny Dignity. The characters that gather around this family may be seen as those parts of the imagination that come to our rescue when needed, are handy, practical and a bit mystical at once.
Cultivating his family garden at the end of the saga becomes, in retrospect a meditation on the nurturing and organic quality of poetry itself, an analogue, perhaps, on-going, pulling all the

action into itself. The journey is one that imagines, that has many cross-currents, several eddies that swirl the waters back on to themselves yet keep a motion forward even with spiralic turns to what was just lived. *Chronicles* offers us all another way of seeing the power of imagination to witness a full life and to lift the ordinary beyond itself, into a flattering and felt sense of what beauty the ordinary moments of life carries always on their back.

Dennis Patrick Slattery
Author, Poet. and Teacher
New Braunfels, Texas
March 2011

Acknowledgments

The work that follows is a story about love, compassion, and genuine human care that takes place in a realm of altruism, a space where one does something for another as much as for him/herself.

I wish to acknowledge the following people who, in one way or another, assisted me in this literary endeavor. My apologies and gratitude to anyone I may omit.

First I wish to thank my father and stepmother who read parts or all of this work in its various stages. I thank them whole-heartedly for their positive re-enforcement and constructive criticisms.

Thanks to my younger brother for his reading of the final draft and our many talks about the work over the years I was engaged with it.

Thanks to Dennis Patrick Slattery for his well written forward.

Finally and most lovingly I must say thank you to my loving wife whom I met and married when this epic was near completion. It is solely through her loving support and critical analysis that this work found a conclusion. It is within our mutual love that I realized the two main characters in the story are none other than her and I, and that I had been writing it for her from the very beginning—a premonition of our finding one another.

Introduction

A very old man, with but wisps of gray hair framing a craggy face, filled with lines that bespoke wisdom, clutching a worn out backpack in both hands, stumbled into my favorite coffee shop one afternoon. He immediately made eye contact with me.

"This is for you." He approached my table and placed the backpack on it, keeping his full weight via his arms atop the pack as he leaned in close. "It is the tale of a strange life, a story of mythical proportions." His voice then dipped several octaves and he continued in deep reverent tones. "I will entrust it to you if you promise that you, and any future readers, read it aloud as you read it through; voices enhance its magical qualities. Declare this oath to me, here and now: I swear that I, and any future readers of whom I am aware, will read this epic tale aloud, more like a play performed outdoors, rather than words spoken under a shroud."

Something in his deep, husky and ancient sounding voice made his oath request seem much more like an order not to be disobeyed, so I repeated the oath word for word. He nodded slowly and a small spark seemed to leap from his eyes. He handed me the backpack, sighed and departed with a smile.

I unzipped the pack and withdrew frayed, yellowed, hand-written papers bound up into a single manuscript. The cover title hooked me:

Jeffrey R. Romanyshyn

CHRONICLES FROM A MYTH-STICAL WORLD

The blending of the words mythical and mystical intrigued me, so I took the volume home and with my wife, read it aloud all night. Who was this old man? We began to wonder if he who gifted me with the work was the main male character. Indeed, could the writings be his autobiography?

You decide?

SECTION I

Awakenings

Part I
Waking Up In A Mystical World

(I)
Waking up in a mystical new world,
Takes my imaginings for a whirl.
I stumble out of bed in this place strange,
And my right knee ligaments I thus strain.

(II)
So upon a window I limp to lean,
And cast my gaze upward: what do I gleam?
For a moment by two panes I'm confused,
Then first fact gained as I clear glass look through.

(III)
Up above me all is wrong with the sky,
And I quickly/easily discern why.
This world's sun: not morning east resident,
It's western rising sans impediment.

(IV)
Even in my imaginative mind,
I can't fathom what beyond this room lies.
Concern is present more than before,
So I dress to exit the bedroom door.

(V)
The wooden hallway stairs scream out loud creaks,
This fact betrays their age as old and beat.
Once outside within this world that seems wrong,
I'm assaulted by crescendos of songs.

(VI)
Celebrations are in progress it seems,
For I see many eyes hint happy gleams,
Though while so many sing, scream out, and shout,
I notice one man who prefers to pout.

(VII)
Ancient looking with hair old country gray,
His face whispers what his voice will not say.
He also knows this strange world is not straight;
As to why, he chooses not to relate.

(VIII)
I sense he too in this world is a guest,
So to question his place I try my best.
With a speed that seems to defy his age,
He hails a horse-drawn coach and slips away.

(IX)
For lack of anything better to do,
Western sunrise, I follow him into,
Taking a lesson from Old Country Gray,
Hailing my own carriage going his way.

(X)
As the horses plod along country lanes,
I compose these lines just to remain sane,
Fiercely hoping this early chronicling,
Will future end-up morphed into something.

Part II
A Realm Soul-y For Mystics

(I)

My horse drawn carriage still ambles along,
I stick out my head to sniff nature's song.
Scents of wildflowers tickle my nose.
I'm glad even here I can smell a rose.

(II)

I call out a question of the coachman,
Where is our final destination?
His reply is amusingly cryptic:
"It's a realm of soul—solely for mystics."

(III)

I pause to wonder about such a place,
Noting the roadside grass looks mowed and raked.
I assume it is a gentle village,
Where no one engages in muse-pillage.

(IV)

Further concerns I may have are soon eased,
When the coachman requests the front gate key.
I notice a sign above that front gate:
"Artists welcome, everyone else must wait."

(V)

Quite a long line touches the horizon,
Though I pass through inner gate sans Sirens,
Where a guard asks a single thing from me:
Compose a poem for my entrance fee.

(VI)

I show him eagerly some of these words,
"Work in progress," hope him I don't perturb,
Since they're the ones I currently compose.
"When I am finished I will let you know."

(VII)

The gatekeeper smiles as he waves me through,
I am glad poetry is what I do,
As the coachman to his horses whistles,
Smartly they step—just avoiding missiles.

(VIII)

Explosions suddenly sound on my left!
Which tells me why the horses smartly stepped:
They were almost hit by missiles of rage,
Hurled by a disgruntled waiting mage.

(IX)

The gate guardians are quick to react:
Grab this wizard—no warning of attack,
Then drag him topside of outer front gate,
Where they hurl him off into empty space.

(X)

The coachman watches the spectacle too,
And he smiles very wide all the way through.
"That will teach him to shoot at my horses.
Don't mess with a town of mystic forces."

(XI)

He whistles again—the horses obey.
"I'm taking you to an inn," he does say.
I reply quickly that's more than O.K.,
Inquiring if he with me will stay?

(XII)

"Of course I will, your destiny is mine;
I'm your human familiar for all times.
Wherever you need go, or just to talk,
I will drive and/or to you will I walk."

(XIII)

He stops the coach by the POETIC INN.
I like this place that I find myself in.
Compared with several places I have been,
It's opposite of punishment for sins.

(XIV)

With a grand flourish that will never bore,
My familiar friend opens carriage door,
Leads me to the owner at the front desk,
Our rooms are ready—moped and neatly swept.

(XV)

Beautiful sea views from each balcony,
Sun light on water—golden alchemy.
For me a large well furnished three-room suite.
Coachman? One room to rest his head in sleep.

(XVI)

I try giving a second room to him.
My new friend politely yet firmly grins,
"Thank you much but one is enough for me."
So I nod and just let the matter be.

(XVII)

He then retires to his one room space,
Where he sleeps till dinner the kitchen makes.
This provides me time to complete these words,
Close of Part II, Part III soon to be served.

Part III
Getting To Know The Village Idiot

(I)
The next morning about the town I roam,
To meet some others who call this place home.
My familiar friend accompanies me,
Since he too is quite curious to see.

(II)
We wander into many a wizard,
Chat with painters, sculptors and chiselers.
Most intriguing? By no means hideous:
Called by others the Village Idiot.

(III)
The reason behind this descriptive phrase,
Is apparent through the artwork he craves.
Many dismiss him as totally crazed,
Since sand drawings are his artistic way.

(IV)
Where on the beach he creatively drew,
Suggests that his brain is not tightly screwed.
Since by the waters he sits himself true,
Where waves wipe away his work-leave no clue.

(V)
The coachman is more than slightly amused:
"Better place for his drawings he ought choose."
In response I shake my head side to side:
"Quite the contrary—he's one with the tide."

(VI)

Seemingly on cue he turns and eyes me:
"Please," he gestures, "Sit with me by the sea."
I withdraw pen—pad already in hand.
"Thank you—I like comparing sea with man."

(VII)

"You are the new poet," he says to me.
"I am. How did you know I write to be?"
He answers "Through your heart the world intones,
Your work offers wandering souls a home."

(VIII)

"Thank you much," I say, "And what about you?
A clue or two why you do what you do?
I must admit I really admire,
How your creation's silicon fired."

(IX)

The Idiot at me slowly does grin:
"You are the first to not call it a sin.
Everyone else believes I'm quite insane,
To watch my work destroyed by tidal rains."

(X)

"I have been awaiting one such as you,"
The Idiot smiles as he continues.
"For together we can join our muses,
To re-ignite burnt out mythic fuses."

(XI)

At my familiar I cast a quick glance,
And his nod compels me to take a chance,
His body hinting a changed position:
"My advice: make his offer your mission."

(XII)
"You live where?" I idiotically ask.
"The POETIC INN," was his reply fast.
"So do I," I blink several times surprised.
"We're neighbors," he replies, "Out and inside."

(XIII)
"It is nearly lunch-shall we?" I suggest.
"For more conversation within the mess."
The Idiot stands up as waves come in,
"Let's drop anchor at the POETIC INN"

(XIV)
In the dining hall we soon sit and eat,
Delicious pasta dish flavored with meat.
Afterwards, I finish these current lines,
Part III complete, Part IV appears in time.

Part IV
Arrival Of Old Country Gray

(I)
The following morning dawns cool and crisp.
Earl Grey tea on my balcony I sip,
Watch sunrise over this world's western lip,
Forward to breakfast—pancakes for a bit.

(II)
In the coachman's mouth a humorous fit:
It's a flapjack whole for the heck of it.
I laugh quietly, so silly is it.
Seated next to me: Village Idiot.

(III)
He drawls: "By the sea I'll be all day gone,
In the sands my artwork will be etched-drawn.
Please do not worry or fret," he does say.
"A new-old friend of yours is on his way."

(IV)
I blink more than twice with total surprise.
The gift of a friend dropped from clear blue sky?
No matter who will be more than o.k.,
Then, suddenly, Inn-walks Old Country Gray!

(V)
A smile broad and wide paint brushes his face,
As he rushes over to me embrace.
I return his affection with great haste.
He says: "I knew this journey was no waste."

(VI)

Claps my shoulder as he sits beside me,
And orders tea: one for him—one for me.
I must ask: "This village: how did you know?"
Gray grins knowingly: "Where else would you go?"

(VII)

I make introductions of all my friends,
To later avoid the need for amends.
"Village Idiot and familiar friend:
Old Country Gray, whose life music heart mends."

(VIII)

Later as we walk and take in the town,
Only once from his face do sights birth frowns.
I wonder what he saw and glance around,
And see that his frowns stem from air-born sounds.

(IX)

We stand near a wizard practice field,
Where many a mage practices to heal,
Though some are controlled by other reasons.
Their thunderbolts do pierce heaven's ceiling.

(X)

I pass quite a long look at my old friend:
"This behavior: might we away it send?"
A slow nod of reply from gray-haired man:
"I am quite sure I know a way we can."

(XI)

We walk further on as I wait to hear,
His best-mused idea of any year:
"Together alone it we cannot do,
We require the help of one plus two."

(XII)
We both know the first two people will be
The coachman and Idiot by the sea.
This presence of a third: I wonder whom?
Gray answers: "You'll dream him as he dreams you."

Part V
My Old Irish Grand Muse

(I)
We soon return to the POETIC INN,
To miss dinner is a bodily sin.
Together with my three friends I thus sit.
This fourth to us will be sent: who is it?

(II)
A friendly hand then gently pats my arm.
Old country wisdom soothes my alarm:
"Quite a journey here from the family farm,
"Please try and be patient," Gray's words do charm.

(III)
We all relax and rest away the day.
I write some verse as shadows slowly fade,
Old Country Gray his Mandolin he plays,
Coachman and Idiot sing time away.

(IV)
Following a delicious supper-meal,
We four on my balcony shadow-heal,
We watch the sun say its eastern farewells,
As to the horizon color it sells.

(V)
After that we all retire to sleep,
To replenish soul so its strength will keep.
I quickly drift off to the land of dream,
Where I'm visited by ancestral gleams.

(VI)

"I assumed sooner or later we'd meet,"
My Old Irish Grand Muse said in my sleep.
He had journeyed through the realms that dreams send.
I exclaim: "You are the fourth to me sent?"

(VII)

Dream-hug reply from my ancestor old:
"A duty we must perform—one quite bold."
"Will you be a dream-force only?" I ask,
"Or worldly solid and whole manifest?"

(VIII)

"Worry not, I will materialize.
Though first my soul had to dream-pass through you,
To preserve our Coat-of-Arms family guise,
I'll see you soon beneath western sunrise."

(IX)

Dawn in the non-dream world is crisp and clear,
Horizon is colored like frothing beer.
I hurry so I may breakfast food choose,
Table seated: my Old Irish Grand Muse!

(X)

My three other friends also join the fray,
Introductions of all I start to say.
From Old Country a quick silencing wave:
"Superfluous! We're familiar all-ways."

(XI)

Old Country Gray then lays out his plan,
To deal with wizards that harm sky and land.
Everyone soon knows the job they must do:
Mine to distract harming wizards, a few.

(XII)
I make my way to the practice field,
Ignoring mages who are there to heal.
I sit myself smack dab in the middle,
Whip out and play my forgotten fiddle.

(XIII)
The other four assume their positions,
Signal waiting to begin our mission.
Meantime I musically fiddle away.
Then a quick hawk cry echoes from Old Gray.

Part VI
A "Myth-stical" Revolution

(I)
Our signal birthed I thus leap to act.
A design that avoids direct attack,
Bodily harm from us we won't inflict,
Since some mages are already heartsick.

(II)
My other four friends also play their parts,
In Old Gray's plan that is really quite smart.
Instead of a frontal body assault,
We target all twisted egos at fault.

(III)
I pluck my fiddle and hope for good luck,
Country Gray his mandolin he strum-plucks,
My Irish Grand Muse produces a flute.
Coachman and Idiot sing songs to boot.

(IV)
We advance slowly—this army of soul,
Never to retreat—onward we must go.
What seemed eternal lasted but moments,
Have we created new art Covenants?

(V)
Of my four friends one shines above the stars,
His melodic voice soaring high and far,
No one did guess a singer him to be:
This Idiotic drawer by the sea.

(VI)
Ever so slowly we seem to make dents,
In hearts and souls of mages wrongly bent.
Through our musical tours of good life,
We seem on the verge of ceasing most strife.

(VII)
A sudden sound like birth of creation,
This time its intention is cremation.
And though he released no painful death scream,
My Grand Muse left this world as a bright gleam.

(VIII)
All of the mages drifted into dream,
Save one who struggles to resist it seems.
Anger fueled from our musical attack,
He shot lightening into Grand Muse's back.

(IX)
Quickly by outraged onlookers he's caught,
And though he struggles it is all for naught.
They bind then drag him to top of front gate,
Where he's hurled off into empty space.

(X)
In our victory solace does take part,
Since we know Grand-Muse died for sake of art,
I look to the sky and say a quick prayer,
To all deities I feel are up there.

Part VII
Ascension Of The Village Idiot

(I)
From deep within my eyes I wipe some tears,
For my ancestor who gave his life here,
So he will be recalled historical,
I think to erect a memorial.

(II)
The Old Country approaches me slowly,
Speaks to my heart quivering like jelly:
"Please, do not grieve so, for he is not lost.
You only lose life's way if it's your fault."

(III)
For now I place personal grief aside,
Crowd's excitement going up from downside.
Since all gathered must make a decision.
The mage hurled lived in the rulers' mansion.

(IV)
An election is lawfully arranged,
All have the vote—a blessing and a bane.
From all citizens we must one be choosing,
Who will rule wisely—not be caught dozing.

(V)
The nominations are out loud declared,
Ranging from bullish men to maidens fair.
I'm seized by an idea: do I dare?
"I think the Idiot for us should care."

(VI)
I felt I'd composed a funeral dirge,
As such total silence followed my words.
I have to wonder if anyone heard,
Then again, no one shouts out: "That's absurd!"

(VII)
Slowly, hands fall together in clapping,
More join in—louder, is it happening?
The Idiot gives me a smile of thanks,
Accepting the duties of his new rank.

(VIII)
Clapping is how leaders are elected.
Our group is one short of a trifecta.
I look at the Coachman and Old Country Gray,
As my smile does say: "Not bad for one day."

(IX)
"The night is still young," Old Country suggests,
"You have an ancestor still to soul-fetch."
Perfectly grasping Old Country's wise words,
I leave them with the Idiot's new herd,

(X)
I find a tree and lean-fall into dream,
My ancestor's there clad in forest green.
I know he is well though he cannot speak,
We'll meet again as western sun dawn peeks.

Part VIII
"Myth-ing" The Point

(I)

I open my eyes to a pre-dawn night,
No people stirring not even a tike.
I sense a presence right behind me, when
My Grand Muse steps back into these word dens.

(II)

"Thank you," he smiles, "For remembering.
Without you, nowhere will I be getting."
I reply: "I am glad you have returned.
When I saw you snuffed out my heart slow-burned."

(III)

We pre-dawn return to POETIC INN,
To grab some quick winks before breakfast din.
But very quickly the morning does dawn,
Reuniting my friends in morning song.

(IV)

Outside, townsfolk form quite a long line,
Asking for the Idiot's ruling time.
I glance with some concern at my sea-friend:
"Perhaps we should, away for now, send them?"

(V)

His quick response is a headshake of no.
"I'm ready! To the center stage we go."
The Idiot listens to all requests,
And to grant their wishes he does his best.

(VI)

Most leave his presence happy and content,
Though I notice some whose hearts remain bent.
They are twisted with anger in their joints,
Who will probably never "myth the point."

(VII)

My Coachman familiar is first to speak:
"Grant the Idiot a few learning weeks.
He is very new to this way of soul,
That he accepted is a large step bold."

(VIII)

Old Gray and my Grand-Muse nod agreement:
"We'll stand by him as counselor-regents.
A fair, just and kind ruler he will be,
Though stern when it is demanded of he.

Part IX
Embracing Remembrances

(I)
So much has happened in so short a time.
To compose all these lines and keep the rhyme,
Is not the simplest of writing tasks,
Though I vow to finish this epic vast.

(II)
I am not in the least bit complaining.
With my friends who are always advising,
We could not ask to live a better realm.
In it we steer a new course from life's helm.

(III)
It pleases me no end to here write-say:
That happily on this wonderful day,
The Idiot of me makes this request:
"Town education is at your behest."

(IV)
To keep peace and prevent stolen booty,
The Idiot gives important duty.
To my familiar responsible friend:
The new High Sheriff once my old coachman.

(V)
My Irish Grand Muse and Old Country Gray,
Design and build a place to sing and play.
The Inn's basement will see no light of day:
AMUSING EVENING'S JAM-SESSIONS CAFE.

(VI)

Of all my friends I thus make a request:
They teach in my university quest.
With magical help from friendly mages,
The doors open much sooner than later.

(VII)

The courses are geared towards remembering:
Mythological-science renderings,
And literary creative writing,
Most ignorance driven into hiding!

(VIII)

The sun descends on the horizon east,
As we five eat a large jam-session feast.
Eat, drink, sing, and play for hours so long,
We nearly sneak up on heels of dawn.

(IX)

Afterwards is when I finish these lines,
Word-etchings of a special charm and kind,
Then surrender gladly to dream's sweet scent,
Glad to be in this world mystical bent.

Part X
From Here To Everywhere

(I)
It's day one of Muse University,
So far there has been no adversity,
Quick to fill up is every single class,
As to the school many made a mad dash.

(II)
My first course: somewhat like a mystery:
It's called: History of Mythology,
And I begin with unanswered question:
"Myth: poetic cultural expression?"

(III)
A pretty maid fair raises a soft hand.
I am enthralled with her blue eyes so grand.
She speaks a voice that is quite like fine silk:
"Myth is the white cow we forget to milk."

(IV)
My eyes blink a caught-off-guard metaphor:
"To say creation has forgotten chores,
Is beautiful," back to her I smile-say.
"Why we're here," she grins. "Milk myth of its ways."

(V)
I look around: "Any more ideas,
Why myth is "scened" as fancy theater?"
A young lad stands up to his full height tall:
"We rely on science to explain all."

(VI)
Class time passes in academic cheer,
My students want more than just to drink beer.
Their first assignment: due in four weeks time:
"Write your very own myth complete with rhyme."

(VII)
To POETIC INN I return for lunch.
Where Old Gray playfully offers a punch:
"How was your first class?" He smoothes his new kilt.
"A blue-eyed maid said: "'Myth: white cow non-milked.'"

(VIII)
Every one of my friends seems quite impressed,
As the Idiot's perception does guess:
"You're smitten with her," he asks, "are you not?"
I nod-smile yes: "From the very start."

(IX)
"Be careful," High Sheriff politely warns,
"Teacher/student mingling can midwife harm."
Irish and Old Gray first nod agreement:
"We're also your heart's counselor-regents."

(X)
"Though if I may say," intones my Grand Muse,
"It is your school to construct as you choose.
Melding of hearts, regardless of station,
Could improve all higher education."

(XI)
Idiot and High Sheriff at me nod,
As I feel the Old Country touch my arm:
"Yes, I believe now's the time!" he declares,
"To put behind us old-world love nightmares."

(XII)

I smile warmly upon all my friends.
Here in this realm we can old life-amend.
I say: "I will tell her how I feel,
Hopefully then my heart she will heal."

(XIII)

My day of love reckoning dawns blue skies;
I sit my office and breathe nervous sighs,
Awaiting with hope the maid's appearance,
So I may confess to her endearments.

(XIV)

She walks in bearing a sun-like smile,
Something I have missed for quite a long while.
She speaks first, her voice like a placid sea:
"My dear myth-poet: Will you marry me?"

(XV)

That very evening we bonded our souls,
We both felt the love move through our hearts bold,
In a ceremony by the ocean,
Now our lives are focused e-motion.

(XVI)

All of my friends played the role of best men,
With the party afterwards heaven sent.
For our honeymoon the maid and I,
With magical help explored cosmic skies.

(XVII)

While this adventure approaches its edge,
A few important things still to be said:
Everyone will live a long, art filled life,
Children are born to myself and my wife.

(XVIII)
To those who read this should you wish to find,
  This place that exists well off the timeline,
  A chance (albeit small) perhaps you might:
  Always remember myth—avoid soul strife.

(XIX)
Though please keep in mind and always recall,
  What's signed above citadel entrance tall,
  For some (if not many) it is their fate:
  "Artists welcome, everyone else might wait."

SECTION II
The Children Shall Lead

Part XI
I'll See Your Wizard And Raise My Twins

(I)
Very quickly five years have now bypassed,
This village that lives on its own time gap,
Many things are wonderful in my life,
I'm focused on teaching and family life.

(II)
Twin kids from God did my wife and I get,
Who at four look like both of us except,
They both sport hair of flowing golden curls,
A most handsome boy and beautiful girl.

(III)
We discovered soon after they were born,
Their intelligence was beyond the norm,
Since at six months old they both walked and talked,
So we did not at learning chances balk.

(IV)
Yesterday was their fourth birthday wishings,
Though at age level twelve they're studying,
For this town a very fortunate thing,
When gate beyond appeared something frightening.

(V)
The wizard who used to rule this village,
Was back with an army to us pillage.
The High Sheriff listened to his demands,
Then said: "Decisions are out of my hands.

(VI)
The ruling Idiot called a meeting,
At the town council, there was no seating.
Everyone unanimously agreed:
Wizard army or not, we must stay free!

(VII)
We were outnumbered, a fact not ignored.
What to do? We sat an hour or more.
From our children, the answer was sired:
Challenge the mage: a baptism of fire.

(VIII)
Their reasoning hooked all instantly,
Though my wife and I were more than leery.
Remember that our kids are but aged four,
But have stepped halfway through the adult door.

(IX)
Everyone gathers close to the front gate,
And watch as my twins their challenge they make.
The angry wizard is quick to accept,
Believing their deaths is but his first step?

(X)
I hold my wife as we watch anxiously.
The mage laughS a sound that is most beastly.
Suspecting nothing from a lad and lass,
When suddenly, in their hands, slingshots flash.

Part XII
2 Stoned Davids vs. A Magical Goliath

(I)
The mage's reaction is a bit late:
He planned a fireball to child erase.
But our young ones for him are way too quick,
With stones from slingshots, the weapons they picked.

(II)
Both of the fist-sized rocks strike his forehead,
Centered is their aim—he falls over dead.
His army is subdued by this display,
Thus very quickly all ranks melt away.

(III)
Our children quickly return to our side,
As from their lips escape small smiles wide.
They desire no pomp and circumstance,
Though they will be honored given the chance.

(IV)
That evening, village center stage upon,
To thus always protect us from strange harm,
The Idiot says they're special sheriffs.
Chances more likely we shall not perish.

(V)
We return home to a festive meal,
Cooked by my wife the scent has much appeal.
Our twin's favorite: pasta—meatballs fist-sized,
Parallel with their rocks is no surprise.

(VI)
Then our gold-curled twins retire to bed.
Soon my wife and I check their sleeping heads.
They doze peaceful—no outward sign that they,
Put their so young lives on the line today.

(VII)
My wife's chuckle kisses me on the cheek:
"They're dreaming about school work due next week."
I smile and teasingly lead her away(s),
To our shared dream-space—though she knows the way.

(VIII)
We lay together feeling safe and sound,
Then a thought in my mind face-births a frown.
My wife asks: "Darling, why the concerned look?"
"I haven't finished the new breakfast nook."

Part XIII
Party Of Eight? Your Nook Is Ready

(I)
The next morning early I do arise,
Softly from our bed, blankets barely sigh.
My wife's body shifts a slight position.
On with my robe I enter our kitchen.

(II)
I set the pot to boil and brew hot tea:
Earl Grey: cream and sugared, naturally.
I sip as I work on the breakfast nook.
Soon my wife appears with a happy look.

(III)
"Lovely," about the cherry oak she says.
"I knew you'd like for it matches our bed."
She starts flapjacks as I clean up my tools.
Final touch: around the nook several stools.

(IV)
Our twins appear looking very weary,
As at the nook they sit-rub eyes bleary.
They are hungry—it's very evident,
For my wife's pancakes that taste heaven sent.

(V)
Then a soft knock upon our front door sounds.
"I'll get it." I joke: "All in seats stay down."
Old Country Gray and my Irish Grand Muse,
On our doorstep look hungry and amused.

(VI)
"Your wife's fine flapjacks: we sniff them cooking."
They peek into kitchen with hope looking.
I laugh: "Enter hungry friends from afar."
They sit with the kids, grandfathers they are.

(VII)
The Idiot and Sheriff join the fray.
My wife smile-serves them without saying, "Nay."
No one speaks about yesterday's events.
We just afterglow revel in its scent.

(VIII)
I glance at the twins a young decision:
"Home-school: the Pax Romana division."
They don't sulk nor to all assembled whine,
More than polite they are two of a kind.

(IX)
"Those kids are special," Old Gray smiles proud.
The Idiot: "Our fortune they're around."
Sheriff complements: "You two raise them well."
"Not easy," says Grand Muse, "Sans magic spells."

(X)
My wife and I both to all do explain:
"No magic keeps this household leveled plane."
My Grand Muse nods: "Complaining I was not.
A fine home here the two of you have got."

Part XIV
Snowy Lab Coats Comet White

(I)
The next week is a special field trip,
To a place the kids love more than a bit:
Astronomer Carl's observatory,
Spheres music played—his conservatory.

(II)
For half the day Carl shows us cosmic themes:
Nebulae's gas that looks like cloudy dreams,
Planets newly discovered beyond earth,
The twins drink it in: new wisdom re-birthed.

(III)
We thank Carl as we pre-evening leave,
When both twins tug the astronomer's sleeves:
"Look through your scope," they say, "what do you see?"
"Snowball comet headed our way," he agrees.

(IV)
"How can you tell?" I ask the science guy,
A man the twins love without being shy.
"How I know, I can't say, just that I do,
Besides, your kids found it first," he says true.

(V)
They again trump a universal ace,
Always they are first in the knowledge race.
Across both their shoulders Carl drapes his arms,
"Can they stay to help me stop comet harm?"

(VI)
My wife says: "Never will we deny them,
The chance to advance from a well learned man."
They both grin and turn towards the telescope,
Where Carl presents them their own white lab coats.

(VII)
For their mentor, the twin's eyes shine delight.
He says, as he helps them into their whites:
"We have but scant little time ahead, right?"
All challenges our twins accept on sight.

(VIII)
To their work parents leave children behind,
With Carl combined they are three strong minds.
We look at naked-eye unseen comet,
If us it hits, no need ask: "whodunit?"

(IX)
Neighbors wave as they pass us on the street.
To avoid panic, to them we don't speak.
"A burden," my wife says, "Knowing what may pass."
"Have faith love," I say, "In a lad and lass."

(X)
Once home I messenger my two friends wise.
Gray and Muse appear not at all surprised,
How they heard they would not to us reveal?
"Secrets," they say, "always protect our heels."

Part XV
Deflecting Cosmic Magic

(I)
Two days later, Carl and the twins have news:
"The comet broke up—somehow it came unglued."
Despite their words they're in a somber mood.
"That's not all," I state, "Pray tell, do not brood."

(II)
They look my wife and I straight in the eyes:
"For such work nothing cosmic was nearby."
My daughter picks up as son takes breaths quick:
"It must have been the work of kind mystics."

(III)
I grasp-gasp at what the twins are saying;
I'm shocked: never knew they had high training.
Of my kid's grandfathers I am speaking,
It's to their muses they are listening.

(IV)
What tips me off is their previous clue:
Mage's' secrets: tell to no one—keep new.
A knock on our front door as if on cue.
Gray and Muse enter with grins that are true.

(V)
To my wife's pasta meal they do sit down,
Always delicious, never cause to frown.
While we eat my family is curious:
Are mage's lives really luxurious?

(VI)
In evening we sit around the fire,
Sans the twins who to slumber retired.
Gray and Muse explain why they tell no one,
Since the comet work is already done.

(VII)
"The two of us do not want accolades,"
Muse speaks for himself and Old Country Gray,
Whose soul-soft voice leaves my wife and I dazed:
"We prefer our grandkids receive praise."

(VIII)
"They will," says Gray, "with the hours put in,
They and Carl, looking for ways to begin,
To avoid universal comet harm."
"The end of all life here," Irish says strong.

(IX)
"Both of you are inspirations this night,"
Says my wife as tears from her eyes she wipes,
"To the twins, who, through you, one day will reach,
The wisdom of life that all of us seek."

Part XVI
Strong-Armed Reality

(I)
With no excitement, a few months pass by,
As I make our home closer to the sky.
A rooftop balcony: star wish for luck.
Wrap around porch—I need help to construct

(II)
Village newcomer—the man I hire,
Seven feet tall by large parents sired.
His strength seems to rival fabled Sampson,
All call him Strong-Hands—heavyweight champion

(III)
It was only a week after our work;
Strange storm beyond town perimeter lurks.
Gray and Muse identify what it means:
Reality is splitting at its seams.

(IV)
An emergency meeting is thus called,
Idiot: "How to plug this waterfall?"
Old Gray then declares: "One chance does exist,
Poetics can reality assist."

(V)
I exclaim: "What in this world can I do?"
"Good choice of words where it concerns your muse,"
My Grand Muse immediately replies.
"Your art can, will, and must shore up the skies."

(VI)

"It will be dangerous," Old Gray admits.
"You must go to the center of these fits,
Only there will your muse thus take effect,
And make worthwhile your upcoming trek."

(VII)

"Though you don't sound sure, seems I'm elected,"
To Gray I say a look quite reflective.
"I ask for company as this I try,
Someone with me while I'm village outside."

(VIII)

On my left shoulder suddenly descends,
Grip strong that says: "Falling skies we will mend."
Strong-Hands stands tall, which for him is easy,
And with him along I feel less queasy.

(IX)

The Idiot offers us best wishes,
As Strong-Hands from my wife gets cheek kisses,
For volunteering to look after me,
So I'm not a branch pruned off family trees.

Part XVII
Red Carpet Treatment

(I)

Early the next morning Strong-Hands arrives,
Though he's un-lonely waiting me outside,
Irish and Gray say: "We're going with you,
To attempt to fix the skies now un-blued."

(II)

I am glad yet I misplace old concern.
"We're not ancient," snorts Gray, "Still years to burn."
Irish says: "Transportation we provide."
At that moment Strong-Hands points to the sky.

(III)

Magic carpet is descending quickly,
Large covered to keep out weather sickly.
The twins—awakened by the commotion—
See the carpet that stirs their emotions.

(IV)

Rare indeed, they are somewhat demanding:
"We want a ride through skies meandering!"
"Ask your granddads," I say, "I can't decide."
They laugh: "When we return, you two may ride."

(V)

I hug my family for it's time to leave.
I will see them again, this I believe.
Inside the carpet is roomy and large,
An Illusion that catches one off-guard.

(VI)
We rise, though it's hard to discern movement,
But knowing would not be an improvement.
Irish pilots while Gray sits besides me.
"Here we go," he states. "Are you muse-ready?"

(VII)
I admit: "I am unsure what to do."
"When it's time," counsels Gray, "you'll see the clue."
All grow quiet as the carpet flies on.
I pray and hope that I do nothing wrong.

(VIII)
After a while Irish says: "We're there."
I ask: "How can we know if here is there?"
At point of no return, my voice is edged.
Strong-Hands smiles slightly as he shakes his head.

(IX)
"Amazing humor at a time like this."
A grin tugs Strong-Hands' lips more than a bit.
I reply: "There was no joke intended."
Strong-Hands says: "My comment is rescinded."

(X)
Gray looks at me then opens carpet hatch.
We're all assaulted by fierce winds that,
Feel birthed from every direction at once,
And buffet us around as if we're drunk.

Part XVIII
Music Of The Spheres

(I)

So loud a noise do the winds generate,
Strong-Hands' yells barely my ears penetrate:
"To your muse, we three will here toe the line."
Gray and Irish nod, it is now my time.

(II)

I'm in the middle of reality.
I have an idea quite suddenly:
I find a place as around me winds scream,
And chant words about ancestral birth dreams.

(III)

Howling winds at my heels keep snapping.
I am so tired I feel like napping,
And even though the desire I fight,
Soon I drift off sheltered in dreamed delights.

(IV)

While in the land of nod myself I find,
Back all the way—the beginnings of time;
For wind to blow against, there was nothing.
All was quiet, till first birth of something.

(V)

I am quite lucid while in my dream space,
Thus I know immediate future fates:
The winds are blowing hard in village time,
Since it resides else-whence on the timeline.

(VI)
Thus the answer does appear to me:
Create a new place for the winds to be.
Do not question me for I do not know,
How and why this dream space told me just so.

(VII)
It seems to be the music of the spheres:
"What artistic songs do you long to hear?
Artist regardless, impulse matters not,
Pick a discipline—choose somewhere to start."

(VIII)
So then I began to pluck my fiddle,
Composing a rhyme much like a riddle.
The winds stopped, they seemed to grasp the meaning:
Blow hard only when life forgets singing.

(IX)
I awake to find myself carpet floored.
I see Strong-Hands securing the hatch-door.
Old Gray and Irish sit at the controls.
I'm so tired I feel 1000 years old.

(X)
"You performed quite well, whatever you did."
Strong-Hands' smile said I'd see my wife and kids.
Both Gray and Irish then called out to me:
"You're a fine poet—amusing indeed."

Part XIX
After Effects Of Spaced-Out Time

(I)
My family is awaiting us outside,
But at our return they look surprised,
Not the fact that all four of us are safe,
Rather, effects on us by time and space.

(II)
"Only a minute ago you four left."
My wife's description causes all to guess:
In every moment of infinity,
It seems, perhaps, that time flows differently.

(III)
Some logic about it all do we seek.
The whole truth we won't know for endless weeks.
The twins climb in the carpet for their ride,
We watch them soar into now clear blue skies.

(IV)
Welcome home breakfast my wife starts to make.
My help she scolds: "Honey, for heaven's sake."
The meal is done, complete with apple pie,
When the kids return from carpeted skies.

(V)
Strong-Hands, Old Gray, and my Irish Grand Muse,
My wife insists that they eat with us too.
Whatever type of food she cooks taste great,
Thus all complement her talent to make.

(VI)

Much later that same night my wife and I,
Sit on our balcony starry-eyed,
Where she confesses deep interest to me:
"I have found my muse in painting to be."

(VII)

I smile: "That's why you've been in the basement."
She replies: "My art has found its placement."
I must ask: "Soon may some of them I see?"
"Tomorrow," my wife says. "Twins, you, and me."

Part XX
Canvassed Fame

(I)
The next day's dawn is a crimson red glow.
My wife sets up some paintings for her show.
That is the reason why breakfast I fix,
And give both our kids cereal to mix.

(II)
To see their mom's work the twins are eager.
It grows as they eat with a quick fever.
Finally my wife, up from the basement says:
"If funny, do not laugh, just grin instead."

(III)
I need not admit I am quite impressed.
My wife indeed has passed the painter's test.
The kids too gaze upon her work with pride,
Amazed that she can make a canvas cry.

(IV)
All her works are originals, save one:
"The New School of Athens" by her brush spun.
The whole family's action is why we laugh:
Walking Plato and Aristotle's path.

(V)
"Look, that's me!" both of our kids exclaim.
They like seeing themselves in canvas fame.
But now it's time for their daily lessons,
While I create a test of 20 questions.

SECTION III

The Possession Of Language

Part XXI
Possession Is 100% Of The Spirit

(I)

That next evening, we have friends for dinner:
Idiot and High Sheriff: no thinner.
Gray, Irish, Carl, Strong-Hands are also there.
I bring up something for all ears to share.

(II)

"Our Cathedral caretakers," I begin.
"What's wrong?" the Idiot asks: "Have they sinned?"
"Perhaps, I was wondering about why,
Their faces from direct sunlight they hide."

(III)

No one gathered knows why this would thus be.
Visit them tomorrow decide do we.
My wife seems concerned as we wash dishes.
"That's not it! They couldn't be!" she whispered.

(IV)

"What my love?" I hang up the drying towel.
"I'm thinking," she said, "They're souls may be foul."
In bed, late that night, I watch my wife sleep,
With her chest breathing a hummingbird's weep.

(V)

I think: Why do they always stay inside?
Why is it no one's witnessed them outside?
Just who are these cathedral caretakers?
Who don't sniff morning bread from the baker?

(VI)
Next morning my wife, Idiot, and I,
Approach the sacred space beneath a sky,
Soul-pitched black it creates such foreboding
Surroundings I imagine souls moaning.

(VII)
The caretakers meet with us, and I say,
They seem normal every step of the way.
An "ear"-e habit the woman did bring,
To our meeting: noisy insect like thing.

(VIII)
My wife noticed this creature was speaking
In the women's ear strange worded somethings,
And thus my wife reacted instantly,
And quoted strange verses instinctively.

(IX)
The buzzing creature let out a wail,
So loud, from lungs so small, far did it sail.
The two caretakers fainted but briefly,
Demon possession banished correctly.

(X)
My wife I asked, as we walked slowly home:
"Those words you spoke, have you read ancient tomes?"
She answered: "Great-grandma taught me, back when,
Banishments: needed again and again."

Part XXII
Be Careful What You Wish For . . .

(I)
Following morning alone I awoke,
To outside sound that was first time evoked:
The new bells in the cathedral tower,
Tolling the time: seven a.m. hour.

(II)
I found my wife in her art studio,
Painting a work that she called: MEPHISTO,
Her name for the demon, which she banished,
Forever frozen—dead on her canvas.

(III)
"You paint him lifelike," I say: "Quite eerie."
My wife answers: "A possession theory.
His largeness means he succeeded nearly,
But we saw and banished him utterly."

(IV)
Suddenly enlightenment in my mind:
"Evil can't thrive where love's knots closely bind!"
"Yes." My wife then asks me passionately:
"Was love before time retroactively?"

Part XXIII
A Loving Mistake

(I)
Week later: my office, memo reading,
A student comes to me with her case pleading.
The wife of a student, she was surprised
His dissertation partly plagiarized.

(II)
"Professor, hold thy judgment," she began,
Guessing what memo I held in my hands,
"If you punish someone, let it be me!"
Her sincere voice, from depths of soul, moved me.

(III)
"My husband worked so hard shun sleep did he,
As writing became sole priority.
I finished typing the night before due date,
It is my fault: the plagiarized mistake."

(IV)
I smiled to put her worried face at ease,
Then said: "Will you back up a second please.
You want to be judged in your husband's place?
My dear, a sign your love for him is great."

(V)
"An honest error to which you confessed,
Eliminates for me the need to guess,
Why his thesis was submitted this way."
I conclude: "Your truthfulness saved the day."

(VI)

"No action will be taken," I sum up,
"You and your husband are people to trust.
Thus I grant him a one-week extension,
To finish his work sans intervention."

(VII)

Her eyes were shining huge droplets of tears.
She stood and hugged me for what seemed like years.
"Thank you, professor," she sniffed. "I just knew,
With this type of problem to come to you."

(VIII)

After she left across campus I roamed,
For a little while then I thought of home.
Lucky are we who have spouses that love
Us so much it requires many hugs.

(IX)

I entered our house to thus find my wife,
Soul excited to tell me her delight.
"Sit down with me darling and have some tea,
For our two kids we will soon count as three."

(X)

I smile at her with amazement and joy.
"I'm pregnant," she says, "A girl or a boy?"
Hug her and laugh: "No twins this time around?"
She smiles: "Just hope this pregnancy stays sound."

Part XXIV
Womb, Heal Thyself

(I)
On the day that my wife first informed me,
She was six weeks into her pregnancy.
During the next eight weeks my heart sang songs,
But abruptly something went very wrong.

(II)
Abdominal pain woke my wife one night,
So intense it was causing breathing strife.
Thus I took her to the village healer,
Who diagnosed it as a strange fever.

(III)
My wife was now burning hot to the touch,
All she asked: "Will this hurt my baby much?"
Herbal medicine quieted her down,
Then healer whispered to me a sad frown.

(IV)
"Seems to me, the source of your wife's sickness,
Is this: the fever stems from the fetus."
"Is she going to die?" I ask with dread.
"No," he cautioned, "but the baby is dead."

(V)
Like falling stars, hit me hard did his words,
Life had pitched my wife a wicked ball curved.
"I'll tell her," unsure just where to begin.
"Take a few," healer sighed. "Then I'll come in."

(VI)

I understood sadly what his words meant:
The fetus must come out else womb is spent.
I kissed my wife and whispered in her ear.
She tried a brave smile, but cried, filled with fear.

(VII)

Healer returned and sedated her more.
Then with a sigh did he his grisly chore.
I did not look as he carted away,
Our child whose life departed us that day.

(VIII)

Healer insisted my wife stay the night.
I strayed not an inch but kept her in sight.
Healer's wife, who was the village midwife,
Watched over our twins—helped them through this strife.

(IX)

Weeks later my wife took a walk alone.
Through the forest, her expression was stone.
Many tried cheering her up—nothing helped,
Till she heard softly whimpered cries for help!

(X)

Through the forest she thus dashed, seeming mad.
Gone from her mind all thoughts of being sad.
Beneath piled leaves she found her answer:
A baby who gripped her like a panther.

Part XXV
When Fantasy Becomes Destiny

(I)

Getting home, my wife took her precious time,
Slow walking forest paths, cooing in rhyme.
On our doorstep the baby fell asleep.
In her arms he felt safe, so no more weeps.

(II)

I heard her as I opened the door strong,
Only to find a baby in her arms,
"Whose child is . . . ?" She silenced me with a look.
Baby slept on—gurgling like a small brook.

(III)

In our room she laid him on our bed,
So gentle, supporting his tiny head.
She whispered, packing pillows around him:
"Over tea I'll tell you how I found him."

(IV)

Minutes later we sat in the kitchen.
With Earl Grey I listened to her mission:
"I was supposed to find him, please hear me!"
"It's a gift for the child we did not see."

(V)

My wife spoke with such great intensity,
Thus I tried to be reasoned sanity.
"This child must have parents, somewhere in town,"
I said, "So at least let us ask around."

(VI)

"We can, but it won't turn up anyone.
He needs a mother: I'm his chosen one!"
My wife's face was a look so credible,
I surrendered to the inevitable.

(VII)

"I'll go report this to the Sheriff now.
He will know of a missing child in town."
I rose to leave till my wife's look stopped me.
She whispered: "Dear, father too he will need."

(VIII)

The twins, from the noise, had now awoken.
Seeing the baby raised a commotion.
"Can we not keep him? O please, please, say yes!"
I smile: "Now he has siblings two, I guess."

(IX)

I then went quickly to see the Sheriff.
No lost child's parents had squawked like parrots.
He said he'd check as he asked with a frown:
"Your wife found him beneath leaves on the ground?"

(X)

I nodded as I grinned most sheepishly:
"She believes finding him is destiny.
Lost to circumstances, our child last—,
Brought this one into her personal grasp."

Part XXVI
Tiny Dignity

(I)
I then thanked the Sheriff, shaking his hand.
Once home found wife and twins drawing up plans:
On our bedroom they've added a nursery.
"Hold on please," I challenged. "Why the hurry?"

(II)
"He needs a place to sleep," the twins replied.
"On a name for him we ought to decide."
My wife's face was a canvas of deep love,
So I sighed and gave in with a soft shrug.

(III)
"A name?" I asked, "A family decision."
"We have one," the twins spoke in unison.
"We really think him it completely fits:
Tiny Dignity: he even sleeps it."

(IV)
To prove their point to our room they tiptoe.
My wife and I see indeed it is so,
For the child shines dignity all his own;
Even asleep like a bright light he shone.

(V)
"He needs milk, I'll get it from the midwife."
Gone quickly—so dedicated my wife.
The baby woke soon after she returned.
She heated the milk, a process just learned.

(VI)
Tiny Dignity just lay quietly,
Gurgling, he appeared to have piety,
Humbled within, knowing the food would come.
When it did I swear he blinked his eyes some.

(VII)
To me the blinks looked just like he had planned,
Communication sans language human.
I rubbed my own eyes suddenly quite tired,
Saw a son my wife and I did not sire.

(VIII)
He drank one bottle then downed another.
"Burp time," my wife smiled. "Job for his father."
First time I've held him over one shoulder;
Soon he burped—then pooped a foul odor!

(IX)
Baby's par for course, so I didn't mind.
My wife took and bathed him in waters fine.
With angelic glows, from his bath he came,
So much so the twins just had to exclaim:

(X)
My son declared: "I want to hold him first!"
My daughter: I'm about to happy burst!"
My wife said: "You both escort him to bed."
Our twins laid him down gently on the spread.

Part XXVII
Potions Birth More Than Emotions

(I)

"For now where will he sleep?" I asked my wife.
She pondered: "The couch in your study, might,
You move it to our bedroom tonight?
I want Tiny Dignity in full sight."

(II)

I agreed: "It's heavy, so help I'll need."
I called Strong-Hands, who came immediately.
He picked up the couch—not using all his might:
"Least I can do," he smiled, "For your new tyke."

(III)

By now, throughout the village word had spread.
"Everyone I asked now knows," Sheriff said.
Gray and Irish, at our house, soon appear.
"How's our new grandson?" they spoke much cheer.

(IV)

Idiot and Sheriff stopped by on breaks,
Offered help if my wife needed a break.
They said, Tiny Dignity, even in sleep,
His light aura shone out from very deep.

(V)

My wife's smile took their offers in stride:
Tiny Dignity: always at her side.
Though Irish and Gray's look had me baffled,
Like they'd won a universal raffle.

(VI)
They, after Dignity had awoken,
Did ask permission: give him a potion.
To this request my wife quickly agreed,
A position for her that surprised me.

(VII)
Early in our marriage we had agreed:
Refrain from magic to meet basic needs.
How Dignity came to us is I guess,
"Magic," my wife whispered: "It's for the best."

(VIII)
To his lips, Irish brought the concoction,
Dignity drank with happy emotion.
At this Gray and Irish seemed satisfied.
"Please keep us posted." They left smiles wide.

(IX)
Before twins to bed, they kissed their new kin,
And laid Dignity on the couch who'd been,
In my wife's arms as sun set east outside,
Where she heard him imitate a bird's cry.

(X)
That event and potion, got me thinking,
I told her about Dignity's blinking.
That he seemed unique: the end of my thoughts.
Still, yet to come, by surprise we were caught.

Part XXVIII
Aging With Dignity

(I)

A month went by—Tiny Dignity grew,
So quite large that he seemed the age of two.
Worried, my wife took him to the healer,
Hopeful he did not mimic her fever.

(II)

To Old Gray and Irish I went to talk.
Did they play a role in what has been wrought?
No! The potion was one of their new ways,
To help kids fight diseases of the day.

(III)

Both of them said, "We had nothing to do,"
"With this child's origin; we have no clue."
I asked: "Did others' magic intervene?"
"We're atop magic crop," they said, "The cream."

(IV)

'What we mean by that," Gray continues,
"When magic is used, we know the venue."
Irish says: "We inspect the location,"
"To make sure its proper divination."

(V)

"That still leaves us with reasons why," I say,
"Tiny Dignity's grown by months in days."
"Again," speak my two old magician friends,
"Like you we're also baffled," they contend.

(VI)

I thanked both of them and slowly walked home,
Wrapped up in thoughts about known and unknown.
Dignity was special—can't deny that,
But from where he came still begged to be asked.

(VII)

I got home in time for a big surprise;
I felt at that moment my mind decide,
To accept things and do as I was told:
Tiny Dignity walked at six months old

(VIII)

He was quite steady on his newfound feet,
As several times he managed small quick leaps.
This exercise quickly made him hungry,
Bottle he asked for—hand gestured smartly.

(IX)

A pretend one by his lips helped us know,
That he was hungry—indeed it was so.
He sat in his chair and drained all the milk,
Spilling not a drop, thus leaving no filth.

(X)

That was the night he slept in his new crib,
Though while building it I did strain a rib.
Dignity seemed to know as for a sec,
He hugged me so sweetly around my neck.

Part XXIX
A Compromising Situation

(I)

I still have a school to run as today,
I have to pick between two resumes:
One would be an assistant professor,
While the other would be an instructor.

(II)

I talked to both candidates separately.
Man: fluent in languages verbally;
Woman: in the humanities well versed.
That they applied together seems the curse.

(III)

For they are both, to our village, quite new,
And I felt that both of their hearts were true.
Sat in my office and thought succinctly:
"Who would inspire students uniquely?"

(IV)

A decision I did not have to reach,
As they came before me asking to speak.
They had arrived together, thus a bond.
Both wanted the same to avoid some harm.

(V)

Compromise to me, they did suggest it.
Hire both they would share the professorship,
Meaning that, each one, half the time, would teach,
All they would need to comfort living reach.

(VI)

A great idea I had to admit.
Human care triumphs over ego's fits.
So I agreed with all their reasoning,
And hired both starting the spring season.

(VII)

When I got home that night I told my wife,
Who said: "A nice way to start a new life."
Her seductive smile put kids to bed.
"Now, on your massages, let's get ahead."

Part XXX
The "Wow" Of Language

(I)
Six months later a very special day:
It was Tiny Dignity's first birthday.
Our twins also had quite a good reason:
Finished 8th grade, ahead seven seasons.

(II)
The next morning was even more special.
The twins began advanced high school level,
And Tiny Dignity spoke his first words:
"I hope from me these words sound not absurd?"

(III)
It was the first time that he had spoken.
We stopped eating, as our hands seemed broken,
With the forks frozen, halfway to our mouths,
Stunned by his eloquence, the twins said: "Wow."

(IV)
My forgotten fork on my plate clattered.
Dignity asked: "Father, what's the matter?"
My wife asked him, as she first gathered wits:
"Darling, how did you learn to speak like this?"

(V)
With an adult gesture he scratched his head.
"The words in me desired to be said."
"Language just enveloped you all at once?"
I asked, so numb with shock I felt quite drunk.

(VI)
"I can't explain," Tiny Dignity smiled,
To mother, spoke her third wunderkind child:
"Thanks for finding me on that fateful day.
Within each other we have found our way."

(VII)
Upon his words the twins did pick up first.
"How'd you know that upon mom grief was berthed?"
Not really saying she lost the baby.
He smiled: "I'll tell all sometime—maybe."

(VIII)
His voice lowered: "One secret all must keep:
Just you four, and others, can hear me speak.
Most will hear from me but gibberish noise,
Till age four, if those who know keep their poise."

(IX)
We felt like we were being lectured to,
By ten ruling monarchs and their moms too.
We shook our heads yes, what else could we do?
Those others he had mentioned—they are who?

(X)
My face Tiny Dignity seemed to read:
For he said: "All close to you can hear me."
On cue, our front door opening sounded.
Gray and Irish: "We're pleased you're astounded."

SECTION IV

For Love & Science

Part XXXI
Deserving

(I)
I demanded: "Just what is going on?"
Old Gray replied: "No need for words so strong."
"I ask you: humor father, if you please."
With eloquence spoke Tiny Dignity.

(II)
To my twins, still stunned, Irish of them asked:
"Would you give Tiny Dignity his bath?"
Clever move, making them responsible,
Yet, out of earshot of adult hassles.

(III)
Once the young ones were away from us gone,
Gray and Irish tried to soothe our alarm.
"We both knew something like this would happen,
From the time that we first him examined."

(IV)
"Did you're potion augment abilities?"
(My wife's motherly sensibility.)
"Oh, no," Gray replied, "Believe when we say,
It kept childhood illnesses away."

(V)
Irish said: "We saw the body and mind,
Of Tiny Dignity: a special kind.
We were not sure how it would manifest,
Where he goes from here: anybody's guess."

(VI)

"His origins?" my wife's voice was formal.
"I found him in the leaves, quite un-normal."
Irish said: "Regarding that we know not.
Just believe that you deserve what you got."

(VII)

On this subject that is all they would say,
As the twins returned with Dignity bathed.
Then, into his crib, straight to bed, he went,
Saying: "I'll retire since day is spent."

(VIII)

Gray said: "Such a wide vocabulary."
The twins: "His IQ: extraordinary."
They then went to bed, bidding all good night,
The mages left me alone with my wife.

(IX)

I sat at the table and rubbed my eyes,
While my wife brewed Earl Grey before sunrise.
We sipped and gazed upon one another.
I said: "You are a beautiful mother."

(X)

Her love look at me could castle wall raze.
"You're a great father," her words on mine glazed.
We walked hand in hand as if in a daze,
And climbed to the balcony to star gaze.

Part XXXII
Attracting A Cure

(I)

Very quickly a year did pass us by,
And Tiny Dignity grew large in size.
The twins were now seven and he was two.
Everyday he seemed to learn something new.

(II)

His vocabulary grew leaping bounds,
Till no more new words were lying around.
So with the twins he began to study,
Having skipped the phase called Silly Putty.

(III)

I continued my writing and teaching;
Into student's souls I'm always reaching.
And most grasp the point sooner or later,
Though one wouldn't even if I paid her.

(IV)

I invited her for afternoon tea,
In my office: her tale—might she tell me?
She wanted to talk and I found out why:
Her parents quite recently had just died.

(V)

Which is how she came to live in our space.
Her parents, gifted artists, knew the place.
Their estate said if they both should meet death,
Here she'd come to a life of peace and rest.

(VI)

Though her fate, she wasn't accepting it,
Holding memories like they owed a debt.
Thus her problem: not mythological.
She required help psychological.

(VII)

That moment chose to knock my office door.
Strong-Hands: wondering about my new floor.
I hired him to replace my old one.
He glimpsed the women and stopped, beauty-stung.

(VIII)

Straight from her eyes shot out a bright light gleam,
So impressed with Strong-Hands physique it seemed.
Then this man, for him, asked something wild:
"Dinner?" he asked her in a voice mild.

(IX)

"If you're cooking, I'd love to," she replied.
Forgetting me she jumped up by his side,
Then recalled: "Join us please," to me, she said.
"Go enjoy each other," I shook my head

(X)

I smiled as they departed arm-in-arm,
I'm no therapist but that cure had charm.
At home I told the tale to my wife,
Who said: "Seems he's found the wife of his life."

Part XXXIII
Astronomical Wisdom

(I)
Astronomer Carl came to have dinner,
Three weeks later though he was no thinner.
We had him over so we could thus learn,
The telescope my teaching extra earned.

(II)
Recently at the university,
We had started night school diversity.
Seemed everyone was in classes enrolled,
On education's value all were sold.

(III)
We set up the scope on our balcony,
Where we wonder about star's alchemy.
Carl pronounced it a cosmic spyglass fine,
When gazed through took the viewer back in time.

(IV)
"One does that anyway with naked eyes,"
Spoke Tiny Dignity, his face skied
So very high with the stars he seemed glued.
Carl chuckled, clearly in a happy mood.

(V)
"You are right TD," he used the pet name,
For Tiny Dignity—our little game.
"The telescope expands the timed distance,
We see the cosmos move every instant."

(VI)

"Cease your tech speak, in English if you please?"
I joke as the twins look down at their knees,
Then asked: "Why, we understood him father?
So say it again, why should he bother?"

(VII)

To my rescue my wife with love galloped,
And gave the twins pretend verbal wallops.
It was a family game that we always played:
I feigned innocence: the kids had their say.

(VIII)

Then, our three kids to bed, my wife hustled,
Leaving me with Carl's wise brain muscle.
"Ten people only can hear TD speak?"
Astronomer Carl's voice: reverent and deep.

(IX)

"Actually, we prefer it this way,"
I said: "Since easier passes each day.
His smart mind is growing by leaps and bounds."
Carl's nod: "His intellect is quite profound."

(X)

"When he gets older, then what will you do?"
Carl's question over often I did brood.
I said: "We will cross that line when we must."
Carl replied: "TD will quite soon I trust."

Part XXXIV
There Is In Truth Much Beauty

(I)
The following week brings great news gladly.
Strong-Hands and the lady he loves madly,
Are getting married—she who graced his eyes,
With a beauty that took him by surprise.

(II)
To stand as his best man Strong-Hands asks me.
Honored, I accept immediately.
For matron his fiancée asks my wife,
Who also agrees with reverent delight.

(III)
In the cathedral the wedding takes place,
Demon safe—no more do they haunt the space.
Pachelbel's Canon, the music they chose,
For their wedding march—it's beauty composed.

(IV)
The reception is held, following the "I do's",
In the "A-MUSING CAFE", revamped new,
Now its own place—angels above the door,
Strong-Hands' marble sculptures that speak much lore.

(V)
On the village western beach it resides.
A space for some to get away and hide,
At least for a time from normal routines,
For even here life can sometimes be mean.

(VI)
Strong-Hands and wife quietly approach me:
"Sorry we never thanked you properly,
For introducing us." I shake my head:
"It wasn't my doing but fate instead."

(VII)
"Nevertheless, always owe you we will."
Strong-Hand's new wife's voice is edged with a thrill.
"We have good news," she addresses the room.
"I'm pregnant—expecting in eight moons."

(VIII)
Cheerful shouts erupt from all throats gathered,
So loud it seems to penetrate matter.
Strong-Hand's wife again regards me closely:
"Our child—named for you," she smiles happily.

(IX)
My wife on my arm falls over nearly,
Wondering if those words she heard clearly.
I'm in shock, hardly feeling my wife's touch.
"Thank you," I say. "Though I didn't do much."

(X)
Strong-Hand's powerful grip then shakes my hand.
"More than you know you have made my life grand.
Soon I'll be a dad and I'll regard you,
Model perfect: for no one is more true."

Part XXXV
Stored Away Earl Grey

(I)
Harboring nothing strange the months sail by,
Till anchored on weathered docks winter skies.
It's time to store necessities away,
Though foodstuffs are not the sole things we save.

(II)
Artistic trading merchants travel here,
Even during the cold months of the year.
From whence they hail: unspoken secrecy,
This fact only deepens the mystery.

(III)
So, through these cold months I brew extra tea,
Stored in jars: Earl Grey naturally.
Jellied jams and fruity vegetables canned,
We have enough till spring reclaims the land.

(IV)
We're now a week away from Christmas Eve,
So we go to the woods to find a tree.
We take seeds as all villagers believe,
To replant what one chops is a good deed.

(V)
Dignity's job: find a nice fertile place,
So our replanting will not go to waste.
He picks some earth near a gurgling stream.
"Here," he says, "bark of life will be redeemed."

(VI)

So prior to axing we plant the seed,
To replace at Christmas time what we need.
Then we did proceed to fell the green tree,
And it was a tall healthy one indeed.

(VII)

With all pitching in we carried it home,
Dignity held up a branch on his own.
We set it up on the enclosed back porch,
Where it would receive light from the sky torch.

(VIII)

We spent some time decorating the tree,
Small village replica kid built beneath,
Using props Strong-Hands carved from wooden blocks.
He does things with wood most others cannot.

(IX)

Then the moment we all looked forward to:
The last ornament must be secured true.
We all smiled at Tiny Dignity,
To place the angel on top of the tree.

(X)

"Hoist me, father, the honor I accept."
Dignity approached me no fear in step.
He held the angel as I picked him up,
Then placed it, making easy what is tough.

Part XXXVI
Universal Tea Time

(I)
Living in this time-tangent village means,
Events we'll see of improbable means,
And taken indeed it seems as a whole,
Over the edge of life we all will go.

(II)
Please pray tell, just what am I hinting at,
Reader curiosity begs to ask?
First I will say that these thoughts concern light,
The star kind we see in the skies of night.

(III)
We had Carl over for dinner you see,
(His open invitation he redeems,
If not more often at least once weekly,
For my wife's great pasta usually).

(IV)
Upon our balcony we all gather,
Breathing the night glowing cosmic matter.
When the youngest one among us, TD,
Clapped and pointed sky high excitedly.

(V)
Our eyes took in a sight to behold:
A brand new constellation with stars like gold.
Its form: a perfect molded teakettle;
This left all, even Carl, quite befuddled.

(VI)
Carl said: "That part of the sky just last night,
I observed and saw nothing of the type."
"Yet there it is," TD spoke, "Plain as night,
Like a tea kettle pouring all its might."

(VII)
"Then that's what we will call it," Carl replied.
"If that's ok since you were first to find?"
That he asked of TD his permission,
Showed Carl's heart grand and full of deep wisdom.

(VIII)
TD's eyes glowed with such reverent pride,
(For, like the twins, he loved this science guy),
All he did: nod his head slightly at best,
Which Carl assumed correctly as a yes.

(IX)
He then bid farewell as he hurried back,
To the observatory to thus track,
This starry teakettle with a clock drive,
Till it eastern set at western sunrise.

(X)
My wife put our three kids down to rest,
Then rejoined me with her head on my breast.
We lay together on the balcony.
She smiled: "Life with you is its own beauty."

Part XXXVII
A Community Of Everyone

(I)
Since the next morning was a Saturday,
My wife and I planned to sleep dawn away,
But the twins woke us to ask if we may,
Eat breakfast at the new Village Cafe.

(II)
So we got up, bathed, and in good clothes dressed,
Exited from our home walking west,
Into sun peeking over horizon.
It created colors most surprising.

(III)
This new Cafe had just opened its doors,
Painted with lion's mouth grinning a roar.
It was so unique in that it was run,
Not by few villagers but everyone.

(IV)
People volunteered to work different shifts,
Two to eight hours, whatever they wished.
Chefs and servers had to work slightly more,
Than the host job which I volunteered for.

(V)
Out of her schedule of family raising,
My wife, of course, agreed to the baking.
Time to make others plump she was taking,
(And still found time to continue painting)

(VI)
Due to my heavy course load of teaching,
(Also university managing),
I chose to café work mornings Sunday.
My wife's time slot would be evenings Wednesday.

(VII)
We sat a family booth by front window.
TD loved his highchair with a pillow.
We all had scrambled eggs and a short stack,
And while good, nothing beats my wife's flapjacks.

(VIII)
The cafe served breakfast all day and night,
Always open it was, dusk through dawn bright.
And judging by the crowd it was a hit:
Communal experiment sans the risk.

(IX)
On the walk home we took a detour slight,
To beach walk beneath west morning sunlight.
Our kids skipped happily across the sands,
Their laughter in my ears sounded soul grand

(X)
With my wife hand in hand I was walking.
I looked deep into her eyes sparkling.
She responded by kissing me deeply,
Then purring my ear so seductively.

Part XXXVIII
The Language Of Unique Love

(I)
When spring finally returned to the land,
It was earlier than most for had planned.
I had twelve jars of left over Earl Grey,
So I gave them to the Village Cafe.

(II)
On the first Saturday of the new spring,
Many spent the day doing the beach thing.
Old Irish and Old Country Gray were there,
And what they saw made them open mouth stare.

(III)
Strong-Hands, his wife, Idiot, Sheriff too,
All saw it and later swore it was true:
A large seagull hovered above the waves,
Making mournful sounds that echoed a grave.

(IV)
Then, quite suddenly, the gull chatter changed,
A happy screech, it pelted us like rain.
A dolphin appeared from waters beneath,
Singing with the gull beat for happy beat.

(V)
Strong-Hands and his wife picked up on it first:
"They are in love," two voices spoke one burst.
To the sea creatures they were referring;
They're unique kind of love seemed most daring.

(VI)
"An original, intriguing display,
Offered up by nature for us today."
Old Gray and Old Irish mused together,
"Here it stops since the gull can't get wetter."

(VII)
The wizards indeed seemed to be correct,
Then an event that no one did expect:
Trusting love—no fear—the gull perched softly
Atop the dolphin singing happily.

(VIII)
We all spent the remainder of the day,
Sitting on sand speaking between each wave,
That spent their might breaking upon the surf,
For a love that seemed to nature adverse.

(IX)
The dolphin with the gull seabird astride,
Spent all the day's sunlight with us nearby,
Till the sun's eastern descent had begun,
Into it they swam—two shadows as one.

(X)
Deep within that night holding my wife tight,
She kissed me long with such passionate might.
No words between us had to be spoken,
Since love we saw left no language open.

Part XXXIX
Gifts From The Heart

(I)
My office at the university,
I take advantage of rare privacy,
Trying to drum up spontaneity,
For my wife's and my anniversary.

(II)
We've been married seven wonderful years,
And it has been joyful, hardly a tear.
Suddenly a plan within an eye blink,
Like two wine glasses it perfectly clinked.

(III)
I hurry home and find our house empty.
Since it's Wednesday no surprise to me:
It's my wife's evening at Village Cafe,
The kids are with Carl till evening next day.

(IV)
Starting door front candle path I set out,
Each one has companion poem about
The many ways my wife I'll always love,
Balcony finished she gets kissed and hugged.

(V)
Sundown I hear my wife front door return,
I hear her gasp when she sees candles burn.
She reads each poem as minutes pass by.
When she reaches me, tears from eyes she cries.

(VI)
"The most loving gift I've ever received."
Her passion filled kiss makes me shake my knees.
I tell her: "Relax on the balcony,
While I go get us both Earl Grey Iced-Tea."

(VII)
"My darling, I have a present for you,
In my studio," her smile sipped the brew.
A cloth hidden painting on her easel,
Is it the one of the kids with measles?

(VIII)
She took off the cloth and I was in shock,
For me she had redone Rembrandt's NIGHT WATCH,
One of my favorites, it's in my top five.
So now it was my turn to happily cry.

(IX)
"I know the exact place for it," I said,
And hung it at dining table head,
Where it will always be contemplated.
By others, my wife congratulated.

(X)
I awoke and slid from bed late that night,
And tiptoed to my study on feet light,
Where I thought by flickering candle light:
Just one more chronicled part—all I'd write.

Part XL
Freedom?

(I)

So here I sit with shadowed company,
Birthed by a candle's luminosity.
For now I rest by a return to bed,
Since there are a few things left to be said.

(II)

Next evening we have mournful visitors,
Idiot and Sheriff with literature,
That concerns itself with evolution
On which the writer is disillusioned.

(III)

A preacher is responsible for this,
And while I dislike the man just a bit,
His manifesto is a call for all
From university a withdrawal.

(IV)

He kept to himself when he first arrived,
Small theology beneath heaven's skies;
Now he speaks and at first I am angry,
Then realize each stews his own gravy.

(V)

"Grave situation," the Idiot spoke,
Gives me copies of what this preacher wrote.
The Sheriff: "Read it over carefully,
Though time is short so please peruse quickly."

(VI)
After I'm done I say to everyone:
"We will do nothing and it won't be fun.
This preacher, for now, has the right to speak;
Those who follow will show their spirits weak."

(VII)
Idiotic nod: "It's all we can do."
"Our hearts will stay true," Sheriff continued.
After they leave I stare into the night.
My wife's look joins me—one of un-delight.

(VIII)
"I overheard," her whisper hugged me tight.
"That's fine love, but is doing nothing right?"
"If you can ask that question," she replies.
"It's a lucky man I see in your eyes."

(IX)
(That is how—this is where) the journey ends?
Why nine, you ask, what about stanza ten?
Aha! I counter, the rub lies therein:
If more to come write here I'll re-begin.

(X)
(For Now?)
THE END

SECTION V
The Riches Of Rags

Part XLI
Out Of Nowhere

(I)

While late one night in my study working,
Decide I did by candles flickering:
I would compose ten more five-part stanzas,
(Perhaps my final writing bonanza?)

(II)

It is good I did as the next morning,
The sheriff appeared with news foreboding:
From nowhere appeared a very rich man,
Who declared he owned all the village land.

(III)

"That is not all," was the sheriff's warning.
"Everyone must be gone by tenth morning."
He then hurried to inform everyone,
While breakfast I made—now a task not fun.

(IV)

Soon my family in the kitchen appeared.
I told them the news that caused several tears.
"The Idiot is reviewing right now,
All legal papers," spoke my furrowed brow.

(V)

He appeared at our house in the evening,
Looking exhausted he spoke with mourning:
"All documents," the Idiot explained,
"Appear in order with Money Bag's claim."

Part XLII
Money Bags

(I)

That was the name we had hung on this man:
Money Bags—since all he cared for was land.
Towards displaced families two blind eyes he turned,
While his third eye not blinded harshly burned.

(II)

Nevertheless I felt I had to try,
To penetrate Money Bag's wealthy pride,
And appeal to (if he had any),
His soul grain of selfless humanity.

(III)

His outer shell was a stone spherical,
Breaking through would mimic a miracle.
I had him read these very chronicles,
I swear relax did his hair follicles.

(IV)

"Others I've hurt I never realized,"
Money Bags spoke as tears fell from his eyes,
He then promised what I did not expect:
"Here I will live and give my monthly check!"

(V)

That's how this village was able to grow,
By quick leaps and bounds without stubbing toes.
Borders were expanded from forests to seas,
Which helped us handle nature's refugees.

Part XLIII
Artistic Storm

(I)
No sooner had we expanded the town,
When the church bells rang out a troubled sound.
All gathered at the village center stage,
Where the Idiot explained nature's rage.

(II)
"A hurricane hit the crescent city,"
The idiot sang a mournful ditty.
"The gates of our village will be open,
To all who share our artistic notions."

(III)
Soon a hundred displaced people arrived,
All skin-soaked by the hurricane's high tide.
Strong-Hands and other villagers engaged,
Building shelters where refugees could stay.

(IV)
I helped coordinate cataloguing,
Refugee information entering,
Nearly all villagers somewhere pitched in,
Thus the process felt smooth as baby skin.

(V)
It took the light of a very hard day,
Though as sun set east home I made my way,
Knowing all refugees were safe and sound.
I entered our home dark—no one around.

Part XLIV
Why The Lights Came Up

(I)
"This is so strange," I thought, "Where are the kids?"
As I spun open the candle jar lid,
So I could to the subject add some bright.
"Surprise!" yelled voices as up came the lights.

(II)
I was stunned as all my close friends I saw,
With joy gathered in my home one and all,
With my children and wife—whom I adore,
More in this world than any peoples four.

(III)
"Happy birthday, I wanted to be first."
Whispered my wife's form clad in a new skirt.
Old Country Gray and Grand Muse hugged me hard:
"Congrats," they joked, "for making it this far."

(IV)
The Idiot, Sheriff, Strong-Hands, his wife,
Embraced me: "We're happy for you this night."
"Make a wish," three kids around me crowded.
"Your birthday treat: Cajun Style Clam Chowder!"

(V)
The party lasted many hours long,
As we played charades, ate, talked, and sang songs.
The time spent was fun and memorable,
Though next day was slightly questionable.

Part XLV
Preaching To A Lofty Choir?

(I)
Morning: my university office,
Grading papers when I heard a ruckus.
Wondered from where this disturbance was born,
Opened my door on a gathering storm.

(II)
I overlook the school's garden you see,
There was the preacher yelling about me.
No one listened to what he had to say,
Thus his words were making little headway.

(III)
A daring idea leaped into mind,
In my deepest thoughts it did quickly bind.
I called to the preacher: "Come up here please?
I believe I can fulfill both of our needs."

(IV)
Several times with much surprise he eye-blinked,
My invitation left him out of synch,
But he climbed the stairs to my office floor,
Looking confused he almost bumped my door.

(V)
"Before you say anything," I began,
"Hear me out—I might not say it again:
You should teach at this university,
We're always open to diversity."

Part XLVI
Family Approval

(I)
"Me? Really?" He could barely speak the words.
I replied: "I admit it sounds absurd?
Though it will allow students to decide:
God with science: linked truth or patricide."

(II)
He shook my hand: "I accept your offer.
This way we will be each other's buffers."
I shook his hand very strong in return:
"Next week begin teaching what you have learned."

(III)
As he left I pondered what I had done.
"It will make the curriculum more fun."
I sighed as I quite gently closed my door,
Thinking the preacher's class would never bore.

(IV)
At home I told the tale to my wife,
Who approved I had done the thing most right.
The twins and Tiny Dignity agreed,
I'd removed wind from the preacher's sailed peeve.

(V)
The sky on that same night lit up with stars,
And their twinkling presence gave me a charge.
So I fell asleep happy and content,
Believing my actions were not wrong spent.

Part XLVII
Facing Questions

(I)
Since the next morning was a Saturday,
My Irish Grand-Muse and Old Country Gray,
Came by to see me in the afternoon,
Right away I noticed their somber mood.

(II)
"That you hired the preacher—we had heard,"
Anyone else speaking would sound absurd.
It had been less than 24 hours,
Since I had altered the preacher's prowess.

(III)
"We are not suggesting what you should do,"
Old Country Gray uttered a literal truth.
"Yet you both think my decision won't float."
My words were a drawbridge across a moat.

(IV)
Both men took my invitation to cross,
This bridge of friendship where we could thus talk,
Freely and openly with no truths off track;
I made tea and we all sat on porch back.

(V)
"We have one question," spoke Irish Grand-Muse.
"To hire this preacher: why did you choose?"
I sipped some tea then stroked my beardless chin.
"Keep him in eye/earshot," answered my grin.

Part XLVIII
Strange Rolls In New Hays

(I)

Quick to fill up was the preacher's new class,
And there existed a few students that
Agreed with what the preacher had to say;
Strange bedfellows for rolls within new hays.

(II)

A new semester in my favorite class:
History's Mythologies: First From Last.
I open with the same answered question:
"Myth: poetic cultural expression?

(III)

Variants on the same answers abound,
Like the ones I received first time around.
Forgetting to milk white cow of nature,
(My wife's answer): still unique in stature.

(IV)

With my wife's permission I now use it,
I admit to impress students a bit,
But also so much more to steer them right,
That expressive metaphors breathe soul life.

(V)

Pass quickly, as usual, does class time,
Though all want to stay and further talk-dine
On the mystical Garden of Eden:
Is it real or just a fable seasoned?

Part XLIX
Growing One's Own Garden

(I)
I arrive at home pleasantly surprised,
To find my entire family outside,
Around our front porch they're garden planting,
I did not know that this they were planning.

(II)
They were nearly finished which thus left me,
With fulfilling the garden's liquid needs,
I watered as we stood and admired,
The work Tiny Dignity inspired.

(III)
About World War II he had been reading,
The Victory gardens got him thinking,
To plant our own and honor in a way,
All heroes who did democracy save.

(IV)
While eating dinner my kids asked of me:
"Complete are these chronicled renderings?"
"For now," I answered, "Though more may follow.
Like good farmland they will not lay fallow."

(V)
That night with my wife I balcony lay
Gazing at stars before hitting the hay.
She whispered: "Long as you live you will write."
I kissed her soft lips: "Honey you're so right."

Part L (50)
New Endings—New Beginnings

(I)
I did decide on part 50 today,
Our lives ordinary, an average day.
My wife painted while the three kids studied,
And I wrote poetry in my study.

(II)
Major celebration that night is held:
Village turns 50 tolled by the church bells.
Basically it was one huge block party,
In each house—one could eat/drink heartily.

(III)
The Ruling idiot—Gray and Grand Muse,
Strong-Hands—his wife—the Sheriff and Carl too,
Stopped by to eat of my wife's fine cooking,
And drink my tea with jars for their taking.

(IV)
For now these chronicles will find an end,
To all readers these final words I send,
I'm upbeat more will follow, however,
Remember none of us lives forever.

(V)
Thank you all very much for partaking,
Of these carefully etched word renderings,
Two-dimension slices of frozen time,
Speaking in multi-dimensional rhymes.

THE END?

I have been writing poetry since 1995; it is one of my main passions in life. For me, writing poetry relieves stress and leaves me feeling content with a sense of accomplishment, feelings that will be passed on to the, hopefully, many readers of this work.

This poetically crafted story has been a labor of love that spans nearly 15 years. It first breathed life as a long poem, grew into a poetic short story, and achieved fruition as a poetic novella (what I call a poetic epic). I was inspired by my historical studies and European travels to write a story that mixes the poetical, mythical and historical with modern reality, a sort of renaissance tale with a mythical, post-modern twist.

I reside in Houston, Texas and am married to a wonderful woman who supports my writings like the wife of the narrator of this story.

On the physical side of life, I have been diagnosed with Parkinson's disease since 1992. I hope that this work will serve as an inspiration to others, especially to those dealing with disabilities. I find it to be no accident of fate that God chose this poetic epic to be birthed a few years later within me. To state it simply, the narrator of this story is I, and I am he. You can communicate with both of us, it's just a question how you do it.

God Bless.
Jeffrey Romanyshyn